LIGHTS OUT!

JOHN HIMMELMAN

BridgeWater Paperback

Published by BridgeWater Paperback, an imprint
and trademark of Troll Communications L.L.C.

First published in hardcover by BridgeWater Books.

Printed in the United States of America.

10 9 8 7 6 5 4 3 2 1

Library of Congress Cataloging-in-Publcation Data

Himmelman, John.
Lights out! / story and pictures by John Himmelman.
p. cm.
Summary: Eyeballs on the ceiling and vampires at
the outhouse are only two of the reasons the Camp Badger
Scouts find for getting Counselor Jim to turn
the lights back on in their dark cabin.

ISBN 0-8167-3450-X (lib.)   ISBN 0-8167-3451-8 (pbk.)

[1. Camps — Fiction.   2. Bedtime — Fiction.
3. Fear — Fiction.   4. Camp counselors — Fiction.]
I. Title.
PZ7.H5686Li   1995   [E] — dc20   93-33811

*For my brother, Jim, and the eyeball on the ceiling
that shared our room.*
                    —J.H.

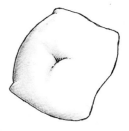

The Camp Badger Scouts were zipped up in their sleeping bags in the dark cabin. "Lights out!" said Counselor Jim. "It's time to sleep." Out went the lights. "Lights on!" shouted Michael.

On went the lights.

"What's the matter?" asked Counselor Jim.

"There's a lion outside the cabin. It's waiting until we are asleep. Then it will leap through the window and eat us, starting with the biggest and saving the smallest for dessert!"

"Is that true?" asked Joseph.

"Of course not," said Counselor Jim. "Lions live 8,000 miles from here. Lights out."

Out went the lights. Counselor Jim went to his room in the cabin. The wind whispered through the trees. *Creak* went the floor.

"Lights on!" screamed Alex.

On went the lights.

"What's wrong?" asked Counselor Jim.

"There's something under the floor. It comes awake in the dark. Then it bursts through the floor and drags sleeping scouts down into its hole, where it makes gross and disgusting noises until they feel sick."

"There is no such thing," said Counselor Jim. "Besides, I have never met anyone who can make grosser noises than the kids at Camp Badger. Lights out."

Out went the lights. The crickets chirped in the cool night air. The moon shone through the window.

"Lights on!" cried Raymond.

On went the lights.

"Now what?" asked Counselor Jim.

"There is an eyeball on the ceiling!" Raymond hollered.

"I saw it, too," shouted William.

"It's hypnotizing us!" cried Raymond.

"We can't move!" screamed William.

"It's just the reflection of the moon," said Counselor Jim. "Now, lights out for real."

Out went the lights. Counselor Jim went to his room. All was quiet. Michael's stomach rumbled.

"Lights on! Lights on!" shrieked Josh. Counselor Jim ran out of his room.
On went the lights.

"Michael is turning into a wolf. I knew he was a monster. I knew it!"
said Josh.

"He does have hairy eyebrows," said Joseph.

"My stomach growled. I'm hungry," said Michael.

"People do not turn into wolves," said Counselor Jim. "Now please try and go to sleep."

Out went the lights. Out went Counselor Jim. In came a mosquito. It buzzed around the room.

"Do you hear that?" asked Joseph. "While we are asleep the mosquitoes will come in and drink all the fluids from our bodies."

"Lights on!" shouted Raymond. In came Counselor Jim. He turned on the lights. He was holding six flashlights.

"Here," he said. "Use these if you need to. But *only* if you need to." He handed everyone a flashlight. He turned out the lights and went to his room.

On went all the flashlights.

"I'm thirsty," said Michael. "I think that mosquito drank all my fluids."

"Let's get a drink," said Josh.

The six Badger Scouts left the cabin and went to the mess hall.

They turned on the lights.

"Someone is coming," said Michael. "Turn out the lights and hide under the table."

In came Counselor Jim. He saw the light from six flashlights coming out from under the table.

"What are you doing here?" he asked.

"The mosquitoes drank all the fluids from our bodies. We're getting a drink," said Joseph.

They each got a glass of water and marched back to the cabin.

"Now, for the very last time, lights out and flashlights off," Counselor Jim said.

Out went the lights. Off went the flashlights. Out went Counselor Jim.

"Uh-oh," said Raymond.

"What?" said Michael.

"I have to go to the bathroom. Will you walk with me to the outhouse?" asked Raymond.

"I have to use the outhouse, too," said Joseph.

"Me, too," said Josh.

Everyone put on their flashlights and left the cabin. A scary bat flew over their heads.

"Vampires! Vampires!" shouted Raymond.

"Vampires! Vampires!" shrieked the scouts.

Counselor Jim jumped out of bed. He looked out his window. "Now what?"

he thought.

"Where are you going?" he asked the scouts.

"We have to use the outhouse," said William. "But it's surrounded by vampires."

"They're just little brown bats," said Counselor Jim. "They only eat those mosquitoes that drank all your fluids."

Everyone took turns using the outhouse. Then they went back to the cabin.

"Okay," said Counselor Jim. "Before I put out the lights, are there any lions outside the window?"

"No," said Michael.

"Are there any monsters under the floor?"

"No," said Alex.

"Is there an eyeball on the ceiling?"
"No," said Raymond and William.

"Is Michael going to turn into a wolf?"
"No," said Josh.

"Are the mosquitoes going to drink the fluids from your bodies?"

"No," said Joseph.

"Is anyone thirsty?"

"No," said the scouts.

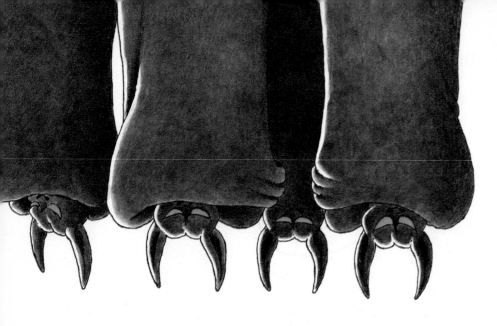

"Are there any vampires outside?"
"No," said the scouts.

"Does anyone have to use the outhouse?"
"No," said the scouts.

"Then for the very, very, very last time, lights out," said Counselor Jim.

Out went the lights.

"Counselor Jim!" shouted the scouts.

"Good night," said the scouts.

"Good night," said Counselor Jim. "I'm going to bed now." And out went the lights.